farer

ALEXANDRA BRACKEN

HYPERION
Los Angeles   New York

For all those history has forgotten.

First Edition, January 2017
10 9 8 7 6 5 4 3 2 1
FAC-020093-16323
Printed in the United States of America

This book is set in 10.5-point Edlund
Designed by Marci Senders

Library of Congress Cataloging-in-Publication Data on file
ISBN 978-1-4847-1576-5

Reinforced binding
Visit www.hyperionteens.com

Not I, nor anyone else can travel that road for you.
You must travel it by yourself.

It is not far, it is within reach.
Perhaps you have been on it since you were born, and did not know,
Perhaps it is everywhere on water and on land.

WALT WHITMAN

LONDON
1932

PROLOGUE

SHE'D HAD A DOLL ONCE, WITH A PAINTED-ON SMILE, AND pale hair and eyes like her own. For a long while, it had been her constant companion—a friend for tea when Alice was traveling with her papa, a confidant when she overheard her parents whispering secrets, someone who had to listen to her when no one else would. Her name was Zenobia, after the desert warrior queen Grandpapa had told her about. But one day, while Henry Hemlock chased her around the garden, the doll had fallen, and she'd stepped on her neck, shattering the fragile porcelain. The dreadful sound it made had sent her heart up into her throat.

Now, the sound of her mama's neck breaking under the heel of the man's boot made her vomit into her hands.

A pulse of fiery power washed through the room like an errant wave, carrying with it all the crushing chaos of the nearby passage as it collapsed. Rose was thrown back against the compartment's wall. The trembling air made her bones shiver, her teeth ache.

Dead.

Rose held her breath, clenching her eyes shut as her papa howled from where the shadowed man had him pinned to the floor, a sword driven through his shoulder. She knew better than to scream with him, to try to reach for her mama the way he was reaching now. The hidden cupboard built into the wall behind the bookshelf would protect her, just as Grandpapa had promised, but only if she stayed *silent*, stayed *still*. The thin crack between the backing of the shelf and its frame was just enough to see through and not be seen.

Somehow the afternoon had slipped into night. Their dinner sat downstairs at the table, nearly untouched—their only warning of the intrusion had been the growls and whimpering of their neighbor's dog before it was quickly silenced. Her papa had just had enough time to light the office's lamps and fireplace, her mama to stow her away, before footsteps fell on the stairs. Now the lingering warmth and glow made the darkness in the room feel as though it was breathing.

"I told you to cooperate." The man wore a fine black overcoat with silver buttons, engraved with some symbol she could not quite make out. A thin black scarf had been pulled up to cover the lower half of his face, but it did nothing to muffle the silky tones of his voice. "It need not be this way. Relinquish your claim to it, give the astrolabe to me, and our business here will conclude."

Broken glass and scattered papers crunched beneath his boots as he circled around her mama . . . her mama's . . .

No. Grandpapa would be back soon from his meeting. He had said he would tuck her in, and he didn't break promises. He would make everything right again. This was . . . it was all a nightmare. It was her silly little mind, dreaming up all those stories about the shadows that came for traveler children. All of this would be over soon, and she would wake up.

"Bloody—*monsters*—the whole lot of you!" Papa tried to pull the sword out of himself by the blade, leaving a smear of blood. The man hovering above him only leaned onto the ornate golden hilt, driving it down further. Her papa thrashed, his legs kicking at nothing but air.

Mama did not move.

The sharp, hot edge of Rose's scream began to tear up her throat.

4

The river of stinking blood had soaked through the rug and was beginning to creep toward her mama's bright hair.

Her father tried to surge up again, one hand gripping a stone paperweight that had fallen from his nearby desk in the initial scuffle. With a yell that ripped from his lungs, he swung the stone toward the masked man's head. The man caught it easily and, in turn, retrieved another thin-bladed sword from the second masked man standing guard at the door. With a grunt, he stabbed it through her father's arm, keeping that in place, too. When her papa let out his bellow of pain, it was not nearly loud enough to drown out the masked man's laughter.

You must watch, Rose thought, curling her knees up toward her chin. *You must tell Grandpapa what happened.*

Stay silent, stay still.

Be brave.

"You—you tell Ironwood that he can die knowing—he'll never—he'll *never* have it—"

Ironwood. Always the Ironwoods. The name was hissed in her family, always edging into their lives like a shadow. Grandpapa had said they would be safe here, but she should have known. They had never been *safe,* not since her aunts and uncles and cousins and grandmother had been stolen, one by one, across the centuries and continents.

And now Mama . . . and Papa . . .

Rose bit her lip again, this time tasting blood.

The other man kicked off from where he'd been leaning against the door. "Finish this. We'll search the floors and walls unhindered." And then, as the figure prowled forward, Rose saw that it wasn't a man at all, but a tall woman.

Her mama had once said that Ironwood liked to collect the girls in his family and keep them on shelves like glass figurines, never taking them down, not even to be dusted. He must have seen this one as unbreakable.

Mama was unbreakable, too.

Until . . . she wasn't.

The first masked man reached into the inner pocket of his coat and affixed a long silver blade to his index finger. It curved like a gleaming claw, pricked at the air.

Rose's eyes shifted away from the weapon, back to her papa's face, only to find him looking at the bookshelf—at her—his lips moving soundlessly. *Be still, be still, be still. . . .*

She wanted to scream, to tell him to fight, to tell him that *she* would fight, if he wouldn't. She had the bumps and scrapes on her hands and knees from tussling with Henry to prove it. This was not Papa. Papa was brave; he was the strongest person in the whole world, and so very—

The masked man leaned down and slid the blade into her papa's ear. His body jerked once more.

His lips stopped moving.

In the distance, false thunder broke against London's sky as another passage crumbled. It was fainter this time, but it still made every inch of her skin feel rubbed raw.

Papa was still there in his suit that smelled of tobacco and cologne, but Rose saw him disappear all the same.

"You start with the bedroom," the masked man said as he wiped the blade and stowed it back in its place.

"It's not here," the woman replied slowly. "Wouldn't we be able to feel it?"

"There may still be a record of it," came the gruff reply, and the man began yanking the desk drawers out one by one. He tossed out ancient coins, papyrus, tin soldiers, old keys, scoffing, "These ingrates are *collectors*."

The woman crossed in front of the bookshelf, making the floorboard squeal. Rose pressed her filthy hands against her mouth again to hold in her scream. She tried not to breathe in the smell of her own sick again, but her parents' blood was already making her stomach churn.

The dark woman's eyes swept over the shelves, and she came to a stop directly in front of where Rose was hidden.

The moment caught in her mind like a leaf on the surface of water. It trembled.

Be still.

But she didn't *want* to be still.

It would be so easy, she thought, to be as brave as Mama—to break through the compartment and try to throw the woman to the floor and run. To pick up one of the swords and slash and slash and slash until she cut the darkness away, the way Papa would.

But Papa had told her to *be still.*

In the corner, the grandfather clock carved out the lost seconds. *Tick, tick, tick . . . dead, dead, dead . . .*

The hot, tangled, thorny parts of herself began to twist around her heart, tightening again and again until Rose finally closed her eyes. She imagined her veins, her ribs, her whole chest hardening like stone to protect the parts of her that hurt so very badly. She was too little to fight them now; Rose knew this. But she also knew that one day she wouldn't be.

The woman's eyes flicked away, toward something on the next bookcase over. Rose let her fear be ground down to pure hate.

Ironwoods. Always the Ironwoods.

"How many place settings did you see on the table?" the woman asked. She backed away from the bookshelves, holding something—a picture frame—out for the man to see. Rose's throat squeezed as her fingers clawed at her dress. That was her papa's photograph of the three of them.

The old house groaned around them. The masked man placed a finger to his lips, his head cocked in the direction of the bookshelves. He stepped over her papa, crossing the distance between him and the woman.

Be still.

7

"We'll take the child," the man said finally. "He'll want her—"

The bang of the front door as it cracked against the entryway's wall carried up the flight of stairs. There was a furious bellow from below—*"Linden!"*—and the bones of the house trembled with the heavy footsteps that spilled up the stairs. Rose looked toward the door just as three men burst through it. The man in the front, his imposing form sweeping in like a thunderstorm, made her recoil. Her papa had shown her a photo of Cyrus Ironwood as often as he could, so she would know him by sight at any age. Know when to run and hide.

One of the men toed at her mama's face. "Well, now we know why that passage closed behind us."

Rose nearly threw herself out from behind the shelf to shove him away, but she realized something suddenly: the masked man and woman were gone. She hadn't seen or heard the window open, nor had she heard the flutter of cloth or their footsteps. It was as if the masked ones had melted into the shadows.

From the shadows they come, to give you a fright.

From the shadows they come, to steal you this night. . . .

"The scum got nothing more than what they deserved," Cyrus Ironwood snarled as he leaned down and yanked the sword up out of her papa's arm, only to shove it down again through his chest. Rose jumped at the sound as the tip of the blade struck bone and wood, felt the soft growl leave her throat.

"This is one bounty I'll *relish* paying," Ironwood said. "I knew it would be the only motivation needed to put this into motion. It's only a damn shame Benjamin wasn't with them—what are you standing there for? Start searching!"

Ten thousand pieces of gold. Rose wasn't supposed to have seen the notice Grandpapa had brought home in a fit of rage. She wasn't supposed to know that Ironwood had put a price on the value of their lives, but Papa didn't—*hadn't* always locked his desk drawer.

The youngest man picked up the same gilded picture frame the masked woman had, only this time from the corner of the desk. He pointed at the picture of Rose sitting primly between her mama and papa. "And her?"

Ironwood spat on her papa's face before he took the photograph. Rose's vision washed over with black, the temperature beneath her skin boiling until she was clawing at her soiled dress to keep herself still. His eyes swept around the room; she could make them out from where she crouched, the color as bright and burning as a lightning bolt. Then, without a word, he returned to her papa's side, crouching down to study something— his ear?

"Boss?" the other young man queried.

"We should leave this place at once," Ironwood said, sounding distracted by his own thoughts. "Take the bodies. We can't risk a change if they're discovered."

"But what about the astro—"

Ironwood spun, throwing the picture frame at the man behind the desk, forcing him to duck. "If the bloody thing was here, it isn't any longer. Now *take the bodies*. I'll be in the car."

He took his poisonous rage with him as he left. Rose let herself breathe for the first time, watching as one man retrieved the pink sheets from her nearby bedroom and, with the other man, went about the business of covering and wrapping first her mama, and then her papa.

The rug was carried out last, leaving nothing but scars in the wood. Rose waited until the front door shut and then counted to ten, listening for something to stir in the shadows. When nothing—and no one— did, she shoved the bookshelf forward and scrambled down the stairs, out the back door. Her eyes stung as she opened the gate, swung her leg over the bicycle that was propped against the fence, and began to pedal.

Rose felt nothing. She pedaled and pedaled and pedaled.

Her vision blurred, hot tears slipping past her lashes onto her cheeks, but it was only because it was so very cold and damp out.

Ironwood's lorry gleamed like the shell of a beetle under the street-lights as she trailed after it, staying back at a distance. All along the way, she remembered one of the fairy tales Grandpapa had read to her, about the man transformed into a monster by his own ugly heart, and she understood it for the first time. Rose imagined her nails turning to claws, her skin to a knight's armor, her teeth sharpening like a tiger's.

Rose had always known it would be a matter of time before Ironwood came back to stamp out the last of her family, but she wasn't like all of those Jacaranda or Hemlock children who had let Ironwood take them in after their own parents gave in, or were executed.

How sad for them, she thought, that they had grown up without any thorns with which to protect themselves.

One day she would take everything from Cyrus Ironwood. She would demolish his throne of hours and his crown of days. She would find him and finish what her mama and papa had started. But tonight Rose would only follow this monster through the shadows.

Because someone would need to tell Grandpapa where Ironwood had hidden the bodies.

TEXAS
1905

ONE

ETTA WOKE TO THE RUMBLING CALL OF THUNDER, HER BODY wrapped in ribbons of fire.

Her mind launched into sharp awareness. The skin was burning off her bones, peeling back to expose every tender nerve and vein to pure, unflinching agony. She choked as she inhaled, her lungs too tight to bring in more than a small gasp of air. She knew she wasn't in water—the ground was stiff and ragged beneath her—but the instinctive flare of panic, the way her body felt heavy as stone as it jerked, felt like drowning.

Etta turned her head to the side and tried to cough up the dust that filled her mouth. The small movement sent a fresh ripple of pain through her shoulder, down her ribs, and then back up her spine.

Fractured pieces of memories burst through the feverish haze of heat and delirium: *Damascus, astrolabe, Sophia, and*—

Etta forced her eyes open, then squeezed them shut again at the intensity of the sun. That single second was enough for her to absorb the image of the bone-white world around her, the way it flickered and shimmered as heat rose up from the pale dust. It made her think of the way sunlight played on the ocean waves. It made her think of . . .

Passage.

13

That was the thunder she was hearing, then. There was no storm coming—no break from the heat. She was surrounded by desert—everywhere, for miles—broken up by distant, unfamiliar plateaus instead of ancient structures and temples. Then this wasn't—

Not Palmyra. The air smelled different here, burning her nostrils as she breathed in again. There wasn't that hint of rotting, wet greens carried over from a nearby oasis. No camels, either.

Her chest tightened, fear and confusion knotting around her stomach.

"Nic—" Even that sliver of a name felt like broken glass in her throat; her dry lips cracked, and she tasted blood.

She shifted, pressing her palms against the rough ground to push herself up. *I need to get up. . . .*

Drawing her elbows in close to her side, she got no further than lifting her neck when the dull pain in her shoulder burst like a blister. A scream finally broke loose, ragged in her throat. Etta's arms buckled beneath her.

"Good God, shriek again a little louder this time, will you? It's bad enough the guardian's on his way, but by all means, bring the cavalry galloping up with him."

A shadow fell over her. In the few seconds before the darkness reached up and dragged her back down, Etta thought she caught a glimpse of bright, almost unnaturally blue eyes that seemed to widen in recognition at the sight of her. "*Well.* Well, well, well. It seems like this Ironwood does have some luck left to his name, after all."

NASSAU
1776

TWO

NICHOLAS LEANED BACK AGAINST THE CHAIR, LIFTING THE wilting corner of his hat to survey the crowded scene at the Three Crowns Tavern again. The air in the establishment was sweltering, giving its rum-soaked patrons a look of fever. The proprietor, a former ship captain by the name of Paddington, was an eager participant in the merrymaking, leaving his sturdy wife behind the bar to coordinate the drinks and meager food service.

Neither seemed to have a care for the fact that the gaudy emerald paint was curling off the wall in clumps, as if eager to get away from the overpowering stench of men deep in their cups. A defaced portrait of George III loomed over them, the eyes and sensitive bits scratched out—likely by men of the Continental Navy and Marines, who had raided the island for munitions and supplies seven months before.

Nicholas weighed the odds, as he impatiently turned his now-warm pint of ale between his hands, that the "three crowns" in the tavern's name referred to the three vices that seemed to reign over it: avarice, gluttony, and lust.

A lone fiddler huddled over his instrument in the corner, trying in vain to raise a tune over the bawdy singing of the men nearby. The knot in his throat tightened, aided by the knot of his stained cravat.

"Jolly mortals, fill your glasses; noble deeds are done by wine. Scorn the nymph and all her graces; who'd for love or beauty pine! Fa-la-la-la-la . . . !"

Nicholas jerked away from the sight of the bow gliding over the strings, lest his mind start chasing memories down that unhappy trail again. Each second was chipping at his resolve, and what patience he had left seemed as insubstantial as a feather.

Steady, he coaxed himself, *steady.*

How very difficult, though, when the temptation to claw at the table and walls to release the bottled-up storm in him had him so close to surrender. He forced himself to focus on the men hunched over their tables, slapping down cards in perfect ignorance of the onslaught of rain pounding against the windows. The dialects and languages were as varied as the ships out in the bay. There were no uniforms present, which was a welcome surprise to him and a boon to the men at the tables around him, as they shamelessly attempted to unload their contraband.

Little wonder that Rose Linden had chosen this place to meet. He was beginning to question whether the woman courted villainy, or if she merely felt at home in it. If nothing else, her choice ensured that the Ironwood guardians watching the hidden passage on the island would not be likely to step in—their sensibilities were too delicate to risk brushing up against the scruffy charm of the seamen.

Settle yourself.

Nicholas reached up to press his fingers against the cord of leather hidden beneath his linen shirt. Against the outline of the delicate earring he'd strung through it for safekeeping. He didn't dare take it out; he'd seen the look of pity and disgust Sophia had fired his way last evening, when she'd caught him looking at it by the light of their small fire, studying the pale pearl, the gold leaves and blue beads attached to the gold hoop.

It was a safer thing by far to keep his eyes forward, rather than fixed on the evidence of his failures.

Etta would find this place agreeable. He could not catch the thought before it escaped, nor could he stop himself from picturing her here. She would have delighted in watching the room, soliciting whatever stories she could about the island's sordid history as a pirate kingdom. He might have lost her, even, to an ill-fated treasure hunt or a smuggler's crew.

Lost her all the same. Nicholas exhaled slowly, packing the ache away again.

On the worst of days, when the restlessness and fear turned his blood to squirming spiders and his inaction became unbearable, his thoughts turned to nightmares. *Hurt. Gone. Dead.* But the very simple truth, the one that remained when every doubt swirled around him, was that Etta was simply too clever and stubborn to die.

He'd purposefully extinguished the lantern hanging on the wall beside them, and he'd ordered just enough small plates of food and ale to allow them to keep their table without question. But his pockets had lightened as the hours wound down, and Nicholas knew that what little pay he'd scraped together from a morning's work unloading cargo on the docks wouldn't keep for much longer.

"She's not showing," Sophia growled at him from across the table.

Nicholas pinched the bridge of his nose, trying to tamp down the swell of frustration before it carried him off.

"Patience," he growled. The night wasn't over yet. "We aren't finished here."

Sophia huffed, downing whatever was left in her pint before reaching over and snatching his, drawing appreciative looks from the next table over as she gulped the remainder of the ale.

"There," she said, slamming the tankard down. "Now we can go."

In his twenty-odd years of life, Nicholas never could have dreamt he'd see the day when an Ironwood looked so utterly disreputable. Owing to the presence of Ironwoods on the island, and owing even more greatly to the fact that the Grand Master himself had likely put a bounty on his and Sophia's heads large enough to purchase said island, they were in disguise.

Sophia had sullenly—but willingly—sheared her long, dark, curling locks to her shoulders, and braided the remainder into a neat queue. He'd secured clothing from a sailor who shared, approximately, her small stature, and she wore it as comfortably as she did her own skin—unexpected, given her past proclivity for silk and lace.

Most surprising, however, was the leather patch over the now-empty socket of her left eye.

Nicholas's fears of her losing her eye after the brutal beating she'd suffered in Palmyra had been well founded. By the time he and Hasan had brought her back to a hospital in Damascus, the wound had become infected, and her sight in that eye was already gone. Sophia had elected for slow death by rot and fever rather than willingly let any of the physicians remove it, no doubt for vanity's sake.

Yet, when they at last had been forced to remove it, some part of her must have wanted to survive, because she had not retreated from life even in the fiercest clutches of agony. In fact, she had healed quickly, and he had to begrudgingly admit her force of will, once she had made a decision, was something to be feared.

It was a lucky thing, too. While she recovered in Damascus, Nicholas received an unexpected note from Rose, left inside Hasan's home for him to find.

Circumstances prevent me from waiting the month out, as discussed. We will meet on October 13th in Nassau or not at all.

At some point during her ride back to Damascus from Palmyra, where they had agreed to their original meeting, something had clearly changed in Rose's evaluation of these "circumstances." Without details, however, Nicholas hadn't the slightest idea if he should be afraid, or merely irritated she expected them to be able to travel so far, so quickly. As sympathetic as he was to Sophia's wounds, the idea that her injuries might cause them to miss their opportunity to discover the last common year had ignited a sickening panic, and no small amount of resentment, in him.

But her bruises and cuts had faded over the nearly two weeks since her beating, until, three days past, she'd been strong enough to begin to navigate them through a series of passages. And, finally, after one short chartered voyage from Florida, they had arrived to find Rose . . . nowhere.

"She's not bringing Etta with her, if that's what's got you looking like a puppy about to piddle on the floor," Sophia said. "Don't you think we would have seen them by now if that were the case?"

He hadn't expected Rose to arrive with Etta, safe and healing from her own wound, in tow . . . at least, not since that morning. Hope, as it turned out, dwindled like sand through an hourglass.

Nicholas forced himself to take a steadying breath. Her hatred of him minced the air between them, and, over the past weeks, her feelings had scarred into something far uglier than he'd known before. It made sleeping near her at night somewhat . . . uncomfortable . . . to say the least.

But he . . . How bitter the word the word *needed* was, when it was attached to Sophia. He *needed* her assistance to find passages, and, in exchange, had promised to help her disappear from Ironwood's reach once their ill-fated adventure was at an end. It seemed obvious enough to him that the true reason Sophia remained with him was because she had not fully given up her designs on the accursed object.

And he had to live with the knowledge of this, because he, God help him, *needed* her. Damn his pitiful scraps of a traveler's education. Damn his luck. And damn all Ironwoods.

"So eager to go back out in this weather?" he asked, narrowing his eyes. She narrowed her one eye right back, then scowled, turning toward the tavern.

Nicholas ran his fingers along the edge of the table, feeling each groove in the wood. Even two days ago, the idea of abandoning his deal with Rose had been inconceivable. Yet, if she couldn't honor their agreement, what tied *him* to it?

You know what, he thought. Discovering the last common year between the previous version of the timeline and whichever this one might be. Etta would have been shoved through the passages, through decades or centuries, until they'd ultimately tossed her out somewhere in that year, stranding her there hurt and alone. He should have fought to flip their aims, so Rose was searching for the astrolabe, and he Etta, but it had struck him, even exhausted and raw with emotion, that Rose would have the contacts needed to quickly sort out the timeline changes.

Nicholas was already preparing for her cold fury when she found out that he had not spent the two weeks searching for the blasted astrolabe, as she'd asked him to. He could start in earnest, once his mind was no longer haunted by his fears for Etta's life. Until then, he would never be able to fully concentrate on the task at hand.

As much as he had, in the privacy of his own heart, toyed with the idea of playing the selfish bastard and disappearing from this story, his whole soul railed against the dishonor of it. Once the astrolabe was found and destroyed, and Etta's future mended, he would be happy to leave Ironwood to his hell of knowing he'd never have it.

But more than honor, more than responsibility, was *Etta*. Finding her, helping her, sorting this disaster out *with her,* the way they were meant to. His partner.

My heart.

He would finish this, and make his own life, as he'd always intended. The traveler's world had never belonged to him. He'd never been granted access to its secrets, or allowed to explore its depth. He'd never been anything other than a servant.

Even Etta's future had been like a distant star to him; he'd marveled at what she'd told him of its progress and wars and discoveries, but it had remained too far away for him to seize, to hold in his heart as something truly real, not wild fiction. Never mind something he could lay claim to. But whether or not they'd go there, or find a home elsewhere, he wanted to restore that world she had known and loved.

The merrymaking in the tavern was occasionally punctuated by the bang of the door, battered both by the force of the storm's winds and the poor wayward souls who stumbled in for shelter. Nicholas returned his gaze to that spot, waiting for the telltale flash of golden hair, the pale blue eyes.

"Can you at least make yourself useful and dispose of the degenerate in the corner?" Sophia grumbled, crossing her arms on the table and resting her head on them. "If he keeps staring at me, I'm going to start charging him by the minute."

Nicholas blinked, swinging his gaze around to each corner in turn, then back at the girl in front of him. "What the devil are you talking about?"

The scorn rose from her like a tide of fire as Sophia sat up from her slouch, nodding toward the far side of the tavern, at a table in their direct line of sight. A man sat there, dressed in a dark cloak, a cocked hat jammed down over his wet wig, as if prepared to bolt out into the storm again at the first opportunity. Catching Nicholas's gaze, he quickly turned back to stare at his pint, his fingers rapidly drumming on the table. It was only then that Nicholas noticed the sigil of the familiar tree stitched in gold thread on the back of his glove.

Something that had been clenched inside his gut finally relaxed. The derelict man was a Linden. A guardian, if he had to guess.

Or an Ironwood trying to lure us out.

No—the past month had made him suspicious, perhaps beyond reason. An Ironwood would have confronted them directly. While his father's family suffered from a drought of subtlety, they were gifted with a rare love of lethality. Still, he felt for the knife he'd slid into the inside pocket of his jacket all the same.

"Stay here," Nicholas said.

But of course Sophia followed him on stumbling, drunken feet. The man still didn't look up as Nicholas and Sophia sat down in his table's empty chairs.

"Those are taken," the man grunted out. "Waiting fer company."

"I believe it's already arrived, sir," Nicholas said. "We seem to have a mutual friend."

"Do we now?" The man turned his pewter pint around in his hands. Turned it again. And again. And again. Until, finally, Sophia's hand shot out and slammed down over it, beating Nicholas to it by a sliver of a second.

"Test my patience further tonight," she bit out. "I *dare* you."

The man recoiled at her crisp tone, blinking as he looked at her face—her eye patch—closely. "That a costume you've got, luv, or just . . ."

Nicholas cleared his throat, drawing the man off that dangerous path. "We were waiting for . . . someone else."

The man's skin looked as if it had been left beside a fire to dry out for several hours too long. It was a familiar texture to Nicholas, one that marked years of working by or on the sea. The man's green eyes flickered across the room as he reached up to tug his hat off and his wig forward.

The man confirmed it as he said, "Saw some . . . let's say I saw some faces I usually try to keep clear of. Scouring the beaches and town real close and the like. Gives a man some second thoughts about help-ing a lady out."

"Can't be too careful," Nicholas agreed. "Where is this lady?"

The man ignored him, continuing in his tetchy way: "Said there'd only be one of you. You seem to fit." His gaze shifted toward Sophia. "Don't know about this one here."

Sophia narrowed her eye.

"She's an associate of mine," Nicholas said, trying to move the conversation along. He could understand the necessity of secrecy, but each second that passed without searching for the astrolabe was a second too long. "Are you to take us to this lady, then?"

The man took a deep drink of his pint, coughing as he shook his head. With one more furtive glance around, his hand disappeared into his cloak. Nicholas's own fingers jabbed inside his jacket again, curling around the hilt of his blade.

But instead of a pistol or knife, the man pulled out a folded sheet of parchment and set it on the table. Nicholas glanced down at the red wax seal, the sigil of the Linden family stamped into it, then back up at the man. Sophia snatched it up, turning it over and shaking the folded parchment as if expecting poison to trickle out.

"Our . . . *flower*," the man said, emphasizing the word, "had other business to attend to. And now I've repaid her favor, and I'll be off to see to my own—"

"Favor?" Sophia repeated, the ale making her even more brazen than usual. "Aren't you supposed to be a guardian?"

The man pushed himself back from the table. "Used to be, before another family killed nearly the whole lot of them. Now I do as I please. Which, in this moment, is leaving."

Nicholas stood at the moment the Linden guardian did, dogging him through the thick crowds until he was close enough to grab his arm. "What other business did she have? We've been waiting for her—"

The guardian wrenched his arm out of Nicholas's grip, bumping into the back of another tavern patron. Ale sloshed over the edge of the pint and onto Nicholas's shoes. "Do I look like the sort Rose Linden would tell her bleeding secrets to?"

Actually, given his rumpled state and the rather impressive scarring around his neck, which could only have come from surviving a hanging, he seemed like the *exact* sort.

"Did she give you *any* other information?" Nicholas pressed, annoyed he had to raise his voice to be heard over the squealing fiddle and the boisterous laughter of the men and women around him. "Is she still on the island?"

"Are we not speaking English, lad?" the guardian continued. "Do I need to be giving it to you in French, or—?"

A feminine shriek broke through the loud roll of deeper male voices. Nicholas spun, searching out the table he'd just left, only to find a serving girl frantically trying to pick up the pieces of several broken glasses that had smashed across their table. Another small figure in a navy coat helped mop up the liquid as it rushed over the edge onto the floor.

"You—you *cow!*" Sophia shouted, snatching a rag out of the flustered serving girl's hand to mop down her front.

"An accident—so sorry—stumbled—" The poor girl could barely get a word out.

"Are you *blind?*" Sophia continued. "I'm the one with one eye!"

"Best of luck with that one," he heard the guardian say, but by the time Nicholas turned back, the man was on the other side of the tavern, and a sea of bodies had filled the space between them. The wind caught the door and slammed it open as the guardian disappeared into the night. The Three Crowns proprietor was forced to abandon a tray of drinks to bolt it shut before the rain flooded in.

"What's this about?" Nicholas asked, moving toward the table. Sophia dropped back into her seat, glowering as the serving girl swept up the last of the glass into her apron.

"Someone," Sophia emphasized, as if that someone weren't standing directly beside them, "decided to be a right and proper fool and waste perfectly good rum by making me bathe in it—"

Truthfully, the liquor had improved her smell.

"I'm not a fool!" The serving girl's face reddened. "I was watching where I was going, sir, but something caught my foot!"

She stormed off before he could tell her it was all right. And, of course, Sophia only seemed further infuriated by her absence.

"What? She can't take a hint of criticism?" she snapped, then yelled after her, "Stand up for yourself, you sodding—"

"*Enough,*" Nicholas said. "Let us have a look at the letter."

Sophia crossed her arms over her chest, slumping back against her chair. "Hilarious. You couldn't even let me hold on to it for a moment before you took it."

"I don't have time for your games," he said. "Just give it to me."

She returned his sharp look with a blank one. A cold prickling of unease raced down his spine.

"The *letter,*" he insisted, holding out his hand.

"I. Do. Not. Have. It."

They stared at each other a moment more; Nicholas felt as though her gaze was slicing him to pieces as his mind raced. He stooped, searching the floor, the chairs, the area around them. The serving girl—no, he saw her kneeling, and surely she wouldn't have hovered by the table if she'd just stolen something. She hadn't swept it into her apron, either. He would have seen that. Which left—

The other man. The one who had wiped down the table.

"Where did the man go?" he said, spinning on his heel.

"What are you on about?" Sophia grumbled, pushing herself back up to her feet. As she spoke, he caught sight of the deep blue jacket he'd seen before, but the wide-brimmed hat did nothing to disguise the slight man's distinct features. The Chinese man stood, watching them from the landing of the staircase leading to the private rooms above. Nicholas squinted through the tavern's dim lighting and took a single, cautious step in his direction. A flicker of a movement, really, but the man bolted with all the ease and speed of a hare.

"Hell and damnation," he groused. "You wait—"

Sophia slid a pistol he had never seen before out from under her jacket, aimed wide, and with a single, careless glance, fired in the general direction of the staircase. The ringing silence following her shot swung the attention of the room toward them. Pistols, knives, and the odd sword rang out and clattered as they were drawn. And with that small explosion of powder and spark, the fight Sophia had been looking for, the one she'd tried a dozen times to get from him, from the serving girl, from whoever so much as looked at her the wrong way, broke out in earnest.

One man, limbs clumsy with rum, elbowed another man in the back of the neck while trying to pull his own weapon out. With a strangled cry, *that* sailor swung his fist around, knocking the first clear across the nearest table, scattering cards, dice, food, and ale in every direction. The card players rose and charged into the nearest throng of gawking men, who were forced, of course, to push back lest they be trampled.

A sailor emerged from the fray, swinging a chair up from the floor, aiming at Sophia, who stood where she was, smirking.

Blind to it, he thought in horror, in that short instant before he bellowed, "On your left!"

Sophia's hat flew off as she jerked around. Her foot rose instinctively, her aim true: the powerful kick landed directly on his bawbles. As the sailor crashed to the floor with a shriek, she relieved him of the chair and smashed it over his head.

The fiddle shrieked as the bow jumped off the strings. The fiddler himself dove to the floor, just in time to avoid a chair hurtling toward his head from a whiskey-soaked doxy trying to hit her rival across her rouge-smeared face.

One lone drunk seaman stood in the center of the chaos, eyes shut as he swayed around in some odd reel, holding out his rum bottle as if it were his dancing partner.

"Damn your eyes!" Nicholas hollered.